IAMPE...

THE GREAT PIRATICAL RUMBUSTIFICATION

WITH PICTURES
BY
QVENTIN BLAKE

The Great Piratical Rumbustification first appeared in *The Great Piratical Rumbustification and The Librarian and the Robbers*, first published in Great Britain in 1978 by J. M. Dent & Sons Limited
This edition first published in Great Britain in 2012 by Orion Children's Books
a division of the Orion Publishing Group Ltd
Orion House
5 Upper St Martin's Lane
London WC2H 9EA
An Hachette UK Company

1 3 5 7 9 10 8 6 4 2

ISBN 978 1 4440 0544 8

Printed in Great Britain by Clays Ltd, St Ives plc

www.orionbooks.co.uk

A STORY
IN THIRTEEN LUCKY
CHAPTERS

The pirates are restless

*

All over town the pirates were getting restless. 'Yo, ho, ho!' they whispered in the lifts, the lofts and the lordly streets of the city.

These weren't the impulsive young pirates, mind you, but the older pirates who had retired from the sea to live on their ill-gotten riches.

That is why they were restless; it was months since there had been a pirate party.

The pirates were longing for Pirate Rum and for steaming bowls of Pirate Stew – a wonderful stew where every pirate puts something good into the pot . . . a turnip, a bunch of carrots, mushrooms, or a bottle of wine.

It is a great piratical delicacy. The sign of a pirate party is a message in the sky – the words 'Pirate Party', written over the stars.

Every night now the pirates studied the sky, but nothing was written there.

'Oh, for a pirate party!' the pirates grumbled ominously, trying their swords for sharpness.

All the pirates – Roving Tom, Wild Jack Clegg, Rumbling Dick Rover, Orpheus Clinker and Old, Old, Oldest-of-all, Terrible Crabmeat – were restless with longing for a great Rumbustification.

The whole city was churning with restless pirates. The difficulty was that a pirate party must be a STOLEN one.

[2]

The Terrapins are restless too

*

Perhaps it was spring, slowly softening the city with pink blossom and little, young leaves.

Perhaps the pirates were spreading restlessness everywhere like measles.

In one particular house in the city there was a particular lot of more restlessness: it was the Terrapin house.

Mr Terrapin was restless because it was a new house, a new big house, a new, big, old house.

It was old in years. It was big in rooms. It was new because the Terrapin family had just moved into it. It was new in the way of being different from the small flat they used to live in.

It had cost Mr Terrapin more than he cared to think about.

When he did think about it, by accident, he turned green and went all limp.

'I must have been mad!' he would whisper to himself. 'I was talked into it.'

The people who had talked him into it were his wife, Mrs Terrapin, and his sons Alpha, Oliver and Omega.

'I'll never pay it off, never!' he would whisper, growing greener and limper at the thought. When he wasn't green he was restless.

His sons, Alpha, Oliver and Omega were restless too, but for a different reason. When they had lived in the flat and tried to do anything adventurous their mother would say:

'*Do* wait my dears, until we have a bigger house. Then you can expand.' (No adventures were allowed in flats, only in big houses.)

Now they had had a bigger house for more than three weeks. Alpha, Oliver and Omega had waited, but nothing had happened, just the ordinary things like bed, school and washing.

A man needs more than washing in his life.

Alpha, Oliver and Omega did their best to make things lively – but they needed cooperation. Their mother tried, but her heart wasn't in it. Their father tried, but if you mentioned money he went green and limp and had to sit down.

The boys couldn't help feeling restless, too.

The pirates, the Terrapins – everywhere restlessness and discontent, spoiling the city springtime.

Then at last, things began to happen.

[3]

Mr Terrapin comes home early

*

Mr Terrapin came home early. He was in a hurry, but he could tell at once that this had been a busy and interesting day for his dear sons.

Someone had painted a pink elephant on his green front door.

Someone had put glue on the door mat.

Someone had covered the door handle with jam.

'Oh, well,' said Mr Terrapin licking his fingers, 'Boys will be boys . . . ah, raspberry – the jam I like best.'

Mr Terrapin climbed nimbly in at the window.

'Darling,' he called to Mrs Terrapin, 'Darling – Millicent! Put on your fur coat, my love, and paint your face. We're going out.'

Mrs Millicent Terrapin was tied to the leg of the table with dressing-gown cords. Alpha, Oliver and little Omega danced around the room wearing warpaint and pyjama trousers.

'Had a good day, dear?' asked Mr Terrapin. 'Now, boys, untie your mother. I want to take her out.'

'You've come just in time, Daddy,' said Alpha. 'Now we're going to set fire to the table.'

'There's no time for that at the moment,' said Mr Terrapin, smiling fondly at his three adventure-loving sons. 'How soon can you be ready, Millie?'

'Well, really, my dear,' said Mrs Terrapin as Oliver ungagged her, 'I don't know if I can. No, no – I can't leave my children just to gratify a wish for a bit of idle pleasure.'

'Get a baby-sitter, Millie,' commanded Mr Terrapin, looking at his watch. 'This is an important dinner. A rich man – Sir John himself – is going to be there. I want to watch him closely and see if I can guess how he made his riches. Ring the Mother Goose Baby-Sitting Service, if the phone is still working. You know they say they had baby-sitters of all kinds for all situations.'

'Oh, of course!' said Mrs Terrapin, looking delighted. 'Such nice reliable people. Perhaps you could ring them while I change.'

But Alpha, Oliver and Omega looked discontented. They did not enjoy having a baby-sitter. They thought they could take care of themselves. However they did not complain or kick the furniture, for they were good boys and liked to think of their mother having a happy evening out.

[4]

Mr Terrapin rings Mother Goose

*

Mr Terrapin rang the Mother Goose
Baby-Sitting Service at once.

A gracious voice answered, 'Mother Goose
here! Who? Who is that? Ah, Mr Terrapin!
And how are your little lads? Good! Good!

And you want a baby-sitter? We have just
the person for you ... Mr Orpheus Clinker, a
naval gentleman, but retired from the sea now.

He will suit your boys, Mr Terrapin. He keeps order, and yet he's full of gentle fun. Yes, he'll be along in a quarter of an hour. Now – as to his supper . . . do you have any rum in the house?'

'Rum?' cried Mr Terrapin. 'Rum? No – no, I don't drink it myself.'

'Ah, well, don't worry!' said Mother Goose. 'He'll no doubt bring his own. Now I must rush! The other phone's ringing. Good night, Mr Terrapin.'

[5]

The baby-sitter arrives

*

A quarter of an hour later a curious hop-and-go-carry-one step sounded on the Terrapin path, and a curious clanging knock fell on the door. Mr Terrapin opened it and peered out.

'Mr Clinker?' he asked politely.

'What's left of him, matey,' growled a terrible voice. The baby-sitter shouldered

Mr Terrapin roughly to one side and stumped into the kitchen.

He wore a long green coat and had a polka-dot handkerchief tied around his head. He had one leg, wooden, and one arm, tin. He wore a patch over his left eye. It did seem that there was quite a lot of him missing, but what was left was more than enough. You certainly would not recognize him as a baby-sitter.

Indeed it was plain to the most shortsighted landlubber (Mr Terrapin, for example) that Orpheus Clinker was a pirate. A large bottle of rum stuck out of his coat pocket. It was so big it weighed him down on one side.

Alpha, Oliver and Omega stared with open mouths. 'At last,' they thought, 'a baby-sitter worthy of us – we deserve him, and he deserves us – what could be fairer than that!' They began to grin, and Orpheus Clinker himself began to grin, a salty fierce grin that ran and flashed all over his face like lightning over a battered sky.

'Well, you're three likely-looking lads, you are,' he declared. 'I thought the breed was extinct, I did.

I didn't consider that there were any of us left among the Younger Generanium. I like the cut of your jib – your jibs, that is.'

The boys were pleased at having the cut of their jibs admired by the man of the sea.

[6]

Mr Terrapin has a moment of doubt and is reassured

*

'Are you a – er – *practised* baby-sitter?' asked Mr Terrapin doubtfully. 'You don't *look* like a baby-sitter. You remind me of something else . . . I'll think of it in a moment . . . of something else . . . ' his voice trailed off.

'Not to say *practised* exactly, matey,' admitted Orpheus Clinker. 'Not actually *practised*, as such. In fact, if you was to force me to utter honesty I'd have to confide that this is the first time the Mother Goose Computer has turned up my card.'

Mr Terrapin's fleeting doubts vanished, as he had a keen respect for machines.

'So you were chosen by computer, were you?' he said. 'Very good, verr-y good.'

He hustled Mrs Terrapin out as quickly as he could, for they were already late for the important dinner, and he was afraid that they might miss the important soup.

Orpheus Clinker reveals his
secret purpose

*

'That's got rid of them,' said Orpheus Clinker, as the Terrapin parents went off up the drive. 'Mind you, I'm not saying a word against parents as such . . . my old mother was a saint in sheep's clothing . . . but there's no doubt that a lot of parents hanging around hamper a man in his activities.'

Alpha, Oliver and Omega nodded and grinned.

They knew just what he meant.

'Are you really a pirate, Mr Clinker?' asked Alpha courteously.

'A really real pirate?' demanded Oliver earnestly.

'A pirate?' squeaked little Omega, like an echo that needed oiling.

'Once I was, lads, once I was,' said Orpheus Clinker with a wistful sigh. 'I'm a retired man now. However, I'm not as retired as all that, and as I look around I can see that this house is just what I need for my secret purposes.'

'Secret purposes?' cried the Terrapin boys, hopeful and thrilled.

'Those who live . . .' said Orpheus Clinker, 'those who live, why they're the only ones who will probably see. For I'm not the only pirate in this city, and this house is crying out for festivity and rumbustification. Come on out into the garden and we'll send a message.'

'A message?' cried Alpha and Oliver, beginning to fizz like fireworks.

'A message?' cried little Omega, beginning to bubble like lemonade.

'Yes, me hearties,' said Orpheus Clinker. 'The smell's right, the wind – why, it's brisk, isn't it? It's salt, isn't it?'

The boys sniffed the air and felt the wind. The wind was indeed brisk and salty, and the air smelled of excitement and mystery.

'Well,' said Orpheus Clinker, 'well then, we'll give a party . . . a pirate party, a Great Piratical Rumbustification – and all the pirates in town will come to drink and dine and dance.'

The boys were struck silent with amazement and delight.

Orpheus Clinker pulled his coat aside to reveal the pistol in his belt.

'I hid it from your parents, lads,' he said, 'for fear that it might cause despondency and doubt. There's nothing like a pistol to bring out despondency and doubt in a parent . . . now, outside, and we'll let it off.'

'Who are we going to shoot?' asked Oliver.

'No one, silly,' replied Alpha, 'it's a distress flare, isn't it?'

'No, lad, no. It's a festive flare,' explained
Orpheus Clinker. 'A pirate-party flare! A
signal for conviviality and rumbustification.
One glimpse of this and all the pirates in
the metropolis will be wiping their boots on
your doormat, (or failing to wipe them, as
the case may be with them as is not brought
up proper.)' Out on the lawn, Orpheus stood
with the boys around him.

He pointed his pistol at the sky and pulled
the trigger. There was a pop like a cork
coming out of a bottle of very powerful ginger
beer. The sky above the Terrapin house was
filled with dazzling green, gold, blue and
scarlet.

'The flares, d'ye see, catch the attention of
every pirate in the city,' explained Orpheus
Clinker. 'The smoke spells out the message.
It's educated smoke, that is. And so the word
gets around.'

The boys shouted and pranced for wonder and pleasure at the sight. Like threads of silver the smoke trails twisted themselves into words, spelling out a message across the stars.

'Pirate Party,' read Alpha, 'Pirate Party.'

'But how will they know where to come?' asked Oliver.

'They're sailors, aren't they?' asked Orpheus Clinker.

'There'll be pirates all over town, a-reading of those lovely words and a-getting of their bearings . . . But we mustn't waste our time. I've brought steak and onions with me. We must begin the pirate stew. Do you think your lady mother would mind if I borrowed her apron?'

[8]

Mr Terrapin feels jealous

*

Across town in a new and startling dine-and-dance establishment Mr Terrapin supped his first mouthful of the important soup. He sighed. The soup wasn't worth all the hurry to get to it. There was something missing. He looked around for the salt but could see none within his reach.

Just then something caught his eye through the big window.

Mr Terrapin looked again. He was amazed to see the sky lit up with stars – green and gold, blue and scarlet – and the words 'PIRATE PARTY', scribbled in silver smoke.

'Someone is having a good party in that direction,' he said enviously. Mrs Terrapin looked too.

'Why,' she said, 'it looks as if it's over our part of town.'

'Nonsense!' said Mr Terrapin, quite crossly. 'No one ever gives a party like that in our part of town.'

'A party like what?' asked Mrs Terrapin,

blinking. (Sometimes she found it hard to follow Mr Terrapin.)

'Like that!' said Mr Terrapin. 'I'll bet there is plenty of salt in their soup ... Why, that doesn't look like a mere party to me. That looks more like a rumbustification, that does.'

He gave another jealous glance out of the window.

Mr Terrapin would have been amazed to find out just how much salt there was at the rumbustification in question.

[9]

The guests arrive

*

The rumbustification wasn't a rumbustification yet, however. Like ragged butterflies, like autumn leaves blown out of hiding, pirates came from all parts of the city to the Terrapin house.

Some came in such a hurry they did not have time to put on their pirate clothes.

They just came as ordinary grey-haired distinguished lawyers and business men. But most of them put on some of their pirate raggle-taggle: their cheerful silk 'kerchiefs, their gold earrings and their cutlasses.

Parrots sat on their shoulders. They played mouth-organs and old brown fiddles as they came. They turned the footpaths of the city into a pirate chain-dance, they turned the streets into a pirate parade.

Suddenly the city seemed to twist and spin and sing like a big humming top. The pirates were spinning it, as they walked and ran and drove back to the Terrapin house. Already the air was rich with the smell of the beginning of pirate stew.

Standing on the steps of Terrapin House
as if it were his very own, Orpheus Clinker
looked like a pirate, a cook and a king all
rolled into one magnificent figure.

As for Alpha, Oliver and Omega, they had tried to dress as pirate cabin boys. They had silk scarves belonging to Mrs Terrapin tied around their heads. They looked like sparrows with the crests of peacocks and birds of paradise.

There was no need for any introduction. With shouts of joy they welcomed the pirates in.

The great pirate party had begun.

Terrible Crabmeat

*

One particular pirate was late, and that was the oldest, wickedest pirate of all. His name was Terrible Crabmeat. He was getting dressed to go to another party altogether when he saw the message in the sky. He was already late for that party too, but then he did not care about manners. When he saw there was a chance of piratical festivity, he changed his mind entirely.

He called for his pirate clothes, his wheelchair and his cutlass. His servant brought him his clothes and cutlass and helped him put them on.

Then he assisted him into his wheelchair (for Terrible Crabmeat was a hundred and five, and rather crippled with age and various kinds of wickedness). This wheelchair was a very expensive one with a motor and a sharp impatient horn. On the back of it was a skull and crossbones, painted by a famous artist.

'Off again!' muttered Terrible Crabmeat with quiet relish.

'Yes, indeed, Sir John,' said his devoted servant (for Terrible Crabmeat went under the name of 'Sir John' to make his wealth seem respectable.) 'I hope you have an enjoyable evening.'

'I shall,' said Terrible Crabmeat cackling with terrible glee, 'I shall. It's been a long time since there was any sort of rumbustification. Ha! I can still make them jump. Yes, they'll still jump when I say jump, or I'll know the reason why.'

So saying he pressed the starter, the wheelchair shot forwards, and off he went – a strange and fearsome figure, heading for the Terrapin house, heading for the Great Piratical Rumbustification which was already under way.

[11]

In the meantime Mr Terrapin
feels disgruntled

*

Mr Terrapin was feeling disgruntled. He got crosser and crosser as the important dinner carried on to its close. Nothing had enough salt in it. The rich man he had wanted to meet, and to observe closely, had not turned up. Mr Terrapin felt he had been tricked, but he was not sure who had tricked him. It was this that made him disgruntled. He longed for the dinner to be over, but it took a long time. Then there were speeches. They were longer. As soon as he could, Mr Terrapin took Mrs Terrapin out to their car and began to drive her home.

'I don't think parties are what they were,' he said as he drove. 'I remember parties that went off with a bang and seemed to fill the air with rainbows and parrot feathers.'

'My dear,' said Mrs Terrapin gently, 'you've grown older since those days.'

'And then Sir John did not turn up,' Mr Terrapin grumbled.

'My dear, he's a hundred and five,' said Mrs Terrapin. 'He's probably gone to bed with a hot water bottle and a glass of warm milk. Or perhaps he was stopped by the police. I'm told he goes very fast in that wheelchair of his.'

'Silly old fool!' snapped Mr Terrapin. He leaned out of the window of the car. 'That's funny! Why is the sky lit up in our part of the city? There's something going on, I tell you.'

A moment later he cried to Mrs Terrapin,

'It's at our house! ... Yes, Millie, it's at our house. Someone has lighted a bonfire on the terrace. Good heavens! The place is full of pirates! Well, that's the last time we ever deal with the Mother Goose Baby-Sitting Service.'

'Now, Henry, don't be hasty,' said Mrs Terrapin, surveying the milling throng of pirates with amazement. 'There may be a perfectly reasonable explanation to all this.'

'Pigs might fly!' exclaimed
Mr Terrapin. But by
now he was as wild
and furious as
the most wild and
furious pirate. For
he could see that the
great pirate party was nearly at its
height. Music flowed like rum, and
rum flowed like music. Every house in
the street was empty. In a great whirlpool
of noise and brightness, the pirate party
had sucked in all the neighbours and
passers-by. Neighbours and passers-
by had changed hats with the
pirates.

You could not tell one from the other,
unless you looked closely, and not always
then.

The noise was tremendous.

But Mr Terrapin was equal to the occasion.
He drove right across the lawn on to the
terrace, scattering pirates right and left. Then
he leaped from the car shouting sternly.

'What is the meaning of this?'

There was a sudden deep silence. No one could think for a moment of any meaning that seemed good enough. Not even a parrot screamed. Alpha, Oliver and Omega who had been dancing a moment ago stopped still, stricken with dismay. They had hoped their father would understand.

'You said we could do something adventurous when we got into a bigger house . . .' Alpha was beginning. But suddenly the crowd parted and out came Terrible Crabmeat, more terrible than ever in his wheelchair.

'The meaning of it?' he croaked. 'It doesn't have to mean anything. This is a stolen party – a peppery, parroty party, a pirate party.

In fact, it's more than a party . . . it's a Great Piratical Rumbustification, and we've chosen you to be our host, Terrapin.'

Mr Terrapin's mouth had opened with surprise. 'Sir John . . .' he began, 'why, Sir John! I didn't realize . . . I didn't recognize you! If you are here, the party must be more respectable than it seemed at first.'

'If you think that,' said Sir-John-Terrible-Crabmeat, 'then you are a noodle. But in the meantime, relax and enjoy yourself. Come and talk to me for a moment. And call me Crabmeat! It's my real name, you know.'

Everyone could see Mr Terrapin suddenly grow easy in his mind.

And then the party began again. It was like fireworks, whizzing and buzzing and going off *bang*, filling the air with rainbows and parrot feathers.

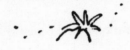

[12]

Now Mr Terrapin enjoys the party

*

At last a party Mr Terrapin could enjoy! Suddenly he became more of a pirate than anyone. He sang and played the tambourine. He did a wicked pirate hornpipe. When the pirate stew was served, he ate three bowlsful. Alpha, Oliver and Omega were amazed and delighted at his activities.

They pointed him out and boasted to people that he was their father.

For his part Mr Terrapin was delighted to hear his three boys so praised and admired. 'They're the right stuff they are,' said Terrible Crabmeat warmly. 'They'll get on in the world, they will. I only wish I had had such spirits when I was a lad.'

When the pirate stew was all eaten, Orpheus Clinker himself washed the stew pot and took it to Terrible Crabmeat. 'Bang on it, man,' cried Terrible Crabmeat in a voice half-croak half-cackle. Orpheus banged on the pot with his hook, causing it to ring like a bell.

'Show your gratitude, swabs!' he bellowed. 'He that calls for the tune, why he's the one that pays the piper, isn't he, now?' He pointed to the empty stew pot he was holding.

One by one the pirates filed past and soon
the yard was echoing to the chink and jingle
of treasure.

Dubloons and pieces of eight fell into the
empty pot. Jewels and pearls sparkled and
shone among them.

'Pirate bells, pirate bells!' said Orpheus Clinker out of the corner of his mouth to Alpha, Oliver and Omega. 'Ring out lovely, don't they?'

'It makes it seem true – pirates-and-treasure,' said little Omega.

'It's been a beautiful rumbustification. Will it happen again?' asked Oliver.

'Will it happen again?' cried Orpheus Clinker. 'Well, I'll tell you this. I've never met three more likely lads than yourselves, as I may have mentioned, and once a pirate, always a pirate. And Great Piratical Rumbustifications always come again!'

'It's the best rumbustification we've ever had,' said another pirate, and Terrible Crabmeat agreed.

The stew pot was filled to the brim. Terrible Crabmeat pointed to it and said to Mr Terrapin: 'There you are, Terrapin, there's cheer for you. It is out custom to make our host an honorary pirate and equip him with treasure. That's your share. Guard it well.'

Mr Terrapin looked at the treasure with delight. He would be able to pay for his house and still have plenty left over. The troubles that had beset him the last few weeks vanished like the merest mist – no more turning green and going all limp. He felt contentment pour into his hear like creamy milk into a porridge bowl.

Mr Terrapin was restless no more.

The pirates had stopped feeling restless, too.

Full of piratical comradeship, and piratical stew, they drifted homeward in the early spring morning, like ragged butterflies, like tattered bright birds. Even the parrots were too tired to screech and flutter.

By the time the sun rose there wasn't a pirate in sight. They were all asleep. They weren't even dreaming.

Mingled with the rumble of cars and buses, was the rumble of pirate snores. It could be heard all over the city. (But you had to listen very closely.)

As for Alpha, Oliver and Omega – they were good for a long time afterwards.

[13]

How it ended

*

Everything had ended happily – almost. Almost, because spring is followed by summer, and summer by autumn and winter. Towards the end of winter, with the beginning of a new spring a curious feeling comes into the city. Most people don't understand it.

'There's a funny feeling in the air,' they say.

But Alpha, Oliver and Omega know what it is, and welcome it with joy.

The pirates are beginning to be restless again.